Just Three Words

Just Three Words

V.C. Linde

Steel Quill Books
An Imprint of NewCon Press

First edition, published in the UK July 2016
by Steel Quill Books,
an Imprint of NewCon Press
41 Wheatsheaf Road, Alconbury Weston, Cambs, PE28 4LF

SQ004 (hardback)
SQ005 (softback)

10 9 8 7 6 5 4 3 2 1

ISBN: 978-1-910935-23-1 (hardback)
978-1-910935-24-8 (softback)

Minor Editorial Interference by Ian Whates
Text layout by Storm Constantine

Contents

Introduction

Kona Macphee

In 1827, Samuel Taylor Coleridge remarked that "prose equals words in their best order; poetry equals the best words in their best order" – an aphorism that's induced irritation in novelists, and a certain smugness in poets, ever since.

It's true that a poet might spend hours, days or even years wrestling with a single word in a poem, striving to replace a self-evidently inadequate placeholder with the One True Word that's really meant to be there. There's nothing precious or self-consciously "arty" about this quest: Coleridge was right about those best words, in the sense that any less-than-best freeloader is a wildly annoying speck of grit in a poem's otherwise clear eye.

If poetry involves the best words in the best order, you'd think that pre-imposing particular words on a poem might be antithetical to progress. (Certainly, having to accommodate "humidifier", "flail" and "phoneme" in a single poem, as Vick Linde did in "Leaving/Living", is a constraint worth of the most expensively stringent Westminster S&M dungeon.) Yet somehow, the principle stands even as the constraints tighten.

The quality that Coleridge's best words have is *rightness*, which produces in the poet (and, we hope, the reader) a sense of inevitability. The poem has always existed; the poet has merely revealed it, opening a previously unnoticed door to find the treasure
waiting behind it. When the starting point for a poem is three given words, the challenge is to discover the whole poem that those words' 'bestness' already belongs to. You may have no idea, initially, what that poem looks like – but you know you'll recognise it when you see it. The three words are keys to unlock the door it hides behind.

For a poet, working with formal restrictions demands a strange fusion of stringency and looseness. On the one hand, the poem has to meet its constraining rules, and this requires discipline and patience. On the other, those same constraints may push the poet beyond preconceived notions of the kind of things they write about, or even the kinds of poems they write. This paradoxical mixture of control and loss-of-control is a heady one, as I'm sure Vick Linde could tell you. Her *Just Three Words* is a journey through many doors, with many marvels to be found behind them. I hope you enjoy the adventure as much as I did.

Kona Macphee
March 2016

Author's Dedication:

For Mr. Robert Kidd.
Would that everyone had such an English teacher.

A Faraway War

Our battle has no guns, no distant enemy
we are armed with peculiar weapons
and hold an unseen line against no one.

Bravery isn't rewarded with medals
but with another ordinary tomorrow.
Another fight. Another morning.

Open sunlight cuts, streams straight onto
our tear-sanded eyes, closed in front
of our quiet secret, our slow war.

Christopher Fowler provided:
Sunlight, Peculiar, Bravery

Christopher Fowler is an English thriller writer. He is the award-winning author of more than forty novels and short-story collections, including the Bryant & May mysteries.

The Dowager

She wears fourteen pearls to bed
and an emerald in the bath.
Unopened bills curl up at the edges
as fires black out the red.
An exquisite life. A hedonistic
escape. She could be anywhere.
Anyone. Everyone knows that
money solves all problems.
Food is delivered in neat boxes,
not just delicate meals but tiers
of cakes and sugared nonsense,
their carcasses litter the rooms by
full ashtrays and half – a lifetime
of dust. Laid over what she once had.

K.A. Laity provided:
Exquisite, Emerald, Nonsense.

K.A. Laity divides her time between upstate New York and Dundee, Scotland. In addition to being an award-winning writer, she teaches medieval literature, film, gender studies, digital humanities and popular culture

V. C Linde

Death of A Snow Bunting

Wings freeze, splinter, shatter, stall in the distant air.
North, beaten North. A tiny keel, turned against
the swirled sky, colour matched to the heading snow.
Black feet, black feathers mark the descent, down, away
from remembered routes. Summer warmth forgotten,
a bliss of heat and ease, green has been undone and
the fall is all there is – down to a calm waste. Nature
lends grace to die. She cannot plead, would not dare.
Each feather breaks into shards, sharp enough, small
enough to cut through flakes. She is not flying, let go,
let down to the trapped landscape. And the matter below
is compacted land, strata of snow, littered with bone,
no contrast, all cold, all clean, all returned to the ice.
Too cold for a grave, the fallen bird remains uncoffined.
She cannot look to her own burial, she cannot protect
her own legacy. The formality of death ends mid-
sentence. Trust placed in nature, faith in the process,
not to leave her corpse lying on the undug ground.
The last thing we own, the last thing we give away,
our eyes – and no longer seeing – we imagine
what is seen. Of us. Of who we were.

Mark Gatiss provided:
Snow, Bliss, Uncoffined.

DEATH OF A SNOW BUNTING.

Mark Gatiss is an English actor, comedian, screenwriter, and novelist. His notable works include writing for and acting in TV series *Doctor Who*, *The League of Gentlemen*, and *Sherlock*, the latter two of which he also co-created.

Gallery

This little girl
stands between
walls of frames,
her eyes skim
paint and pencil
landing, lingering
on a plinth.

She turns away
from painted scenes
to the child of stone.
Carved face
and figure formed from
frangipane-coloured marble.
Toes as hard as thought,
the surface of skin soft
as the inside of her lip.
One still, cool
one breathing, warm.
Friendship fixed quietly,
solid sorority marked
inside their veins.

This little girl
looks up
to face
her silent friend.

Nicola Vincent-Abnett provided:
Sorority, Plinth, Frangipane.

Nik Abnett writes short stories, novels, computer games and comic books, often in collaboration with her partner Dan Abnett. Nik was runner-up for the inaugural Mslexia novel writing prize, and her first solo original novel *Savant* will be published by Solaris in 2016.

When shown 'Gallery', she said:
"I'm rather delighted by the poem, particularly as a maker and collector of art. How very clever!"

Beacon

Dear stranger,
send on this message
in the lambent fire:
"No I shall not come."

Blue words in scarlet flame,
I have only a warning to give
when aid was sought,
no help held within
these hopeless words.

Solace lost with my dispatch,
now yours. Passed along
from one high point
to the next.
A letter sent, its contents graver
framed by the mountains.

Will you wonder who she was,
will you know what she asked,
will you think the worst of me,
the best of her?

My answer limned in the flicker
and the flash of light
against darkening clouds.

Yours,

Zoë Marriott provided:
Limned, Lambent, Scarlet.

Zoë Marriott is author of *The Swan Kingdom*, *Shadows on the Moon*, and many other fantasy novels for children and young adults.

Leaving/Living

Lying to yourself, by the same man again. Curtains flail,
one side pulled down off the rail. Late light comes through.
Another morning of living.
Smoke-washed wallpaper wraps around the room. A border.
One humidifier in a deep house. Chilled without the child.
A vowel, a phoneme, the smallest part changes.
Another mourning not leaving.
Piles of dull dolls. Left behind her.
Pyres of lost lust. Right behind her.
The routine of choices. Dance around what I say, you see.
You know now. No one won.
No difference in between. Gone. Done. Lone. None.

China Miéville provided:
Humidifier, Flail, Phoneme.

China Miéville is an author living and working in London. He has won the prestigious Arthur C. Clarke Award on three separate occasions, along with Hugo, World Fantasy, BSFA, British Fantasy and some half dozen Locus Awards. Having established himself with the SF-tinged urban fantasy of the New Crobuzon novels, his work has subsequently explored science fiction, YA fiction, and weird thrillers.

#

Two people stand
back to back
joined at their spine
A line on the mirror
his face warped
Smudged stars slide
far over
the green canopy
No one near
no one to hear
him
Looking
for a way out
A fresh offering
blood
taken from skin
leaving his face
pale
The crystal
inclusions
clear the view
tell him what to do
The answers come
to him
as smoke twists
the rictus dance
in the wind.

Nancy Kress provided:
Crystal, Blood, Green.

Nancy Kress is the author of thirty-three books, including twenty-six novels, four collections of short stories, and three books on writing. Her work has won six Nebulas, two Hugos, a Sturgeon, and the John W. Campbell Memorial Award. Her most recent works are the Nebula-winning *Yesterday's Kin* (Tachyon, 2014) and *The Best of Nancy Kress* (Subterranean, 2015). Her work has been translated into Swedish, Danish, French, Italian, German, Spanish, Polish, Croatian, Lithuanian, Bulgarian, Romanian, Japanese, Chinese, Korean, Hebrew, Russian, and Klingon, none of which she can read.

Snapshots

Behind closed doors
she fastens on a smile,
frozen, familiar to voyeurs
who follow but never find her.

One step in front of the other,
bare-foot down a grand arched stair.
Flashes shine xanthic light
onto her camouflage, barely there.

Her gelid expression, face down,
not watching the crowds watching
the next step down.

She looks good,
for her age. Damned
with fainting praise.

Eyes up, meet yours.
No, not you. You.
A trick of the limelight.

As she smiles her face breaks
into a craquelure cliché,
over a candid background.
The where and when. Who
she was beneath the paint.

Alan Moore provided:
Gelid, Xanthic, Craquelure.

Alan Moore is an English writer primarily known for his work in graphic novels. A resident and fierce champion of the town of Northampton, he is widely held to be the best graphic novel writer in history. Despite his objections, his work has been adapted for several Hollywood films: *From Hell* (2001), *The League of Extraordinary Gentlemen* (2003), *V for Vendetta* (2005), and *Watchmen* (2009). Moore has also been referenced in popular culture and is acknowledged as an influence by a variety of literary and television figures including Neil Gaiman, Joss Whedon, and Damon Lindelof.

V. C Linde

Orphanage

Fifty-two beds against two walls,
creaking frames on splintered boards,
faces once moonlit are shadow
and bone, skull replaced skin.
Bricked up and locked inside
pace the rows, feet slow, blind
inside a windowless room.

The empty ones will tell their story.
Pillows dented where small heads rested.
Caught in a web and kept in a cage,
until he vanished, relief at first
and then water dried and the food spoiled
and one by one they faded.
Children left behind, remains, their closed eyes
never flicker. Kept, stored, ready for use.
Obsolete they lay in place,
time moves on and they lie still.
Reach out to touch, turn to dust.

Ramsey Campbell provided:
Blind, Moonlit, Children.

Ramsey Campbell has been writing horror for more than fifty years. He has been described variously as "Britain's most respected living horror writer" (*Oxford Companion to English Literature*), "every bit the equal of Lovecraft or Blackwood" (S.T. Joshi) and "perhaps the finest living exponent of the British weird fiction tradition" (Robert Hadji). Campbell's work has won numerous awards and accolades and has been adapted for both film and TV.

When shown "Orphanage", he commented:
"Lord, that's insidiously disturbing. I'm more than happy to have provided the seed!"

V. C Linde

Written In Stone

Faith carved in two rocks –
sandstone and emerald
one a monument and one a talisman.

Inclusions split the light. A different view
looking from East, from West. An invocation
to teach curled inside carved promises.

Two sides – opposing voices
not raised in anger but relief. They last
beyond their makers.
Built to protect and to pray.

Tanith Lee provided:
Emerald, Anger, Monument.

Tanith Lee (1947 – 2015) was one of the UK's most respected authors of fantasy and science fiction, with some hundred novels and over three hundred short stories to her credit. She also scripted two episodes of the iconic TV series *Blake's 7*.

Shown "Written in Stone" a few months prior to her passing, Tanith asked that the following should be forwarded the author: "Vicks poem is tremendous. Very atmospheric."

On Point

Blood soaks the dancers' toes.
Snow white shoes with rose-red blood.

Drip sweat through the days
before curtains lift
into position for the first night

when they earn our tears
with theirs.

Joe Abercrombie provided:
Blood, Sweat, Tears.

Joe Abercrombie is a British fantasy writer and film editor. One of the pioneers of 'grim-dark' fantasy, he is the best-selling author of The First Law trilogy and associated novels, beginning with *Best Served Cold* (2006), and the Shattered Sea series.

Swan Song

Hold my fingers tightly in yours
bring them up to your lips and
let your breath play a sweet tune
on that flute of hollowed bones.
Cut off a spiral lock of hair
and wear it as a ring, strands
tight twisted with sweat where I
writhed when you cut into me.
Pull out my nails one by one
to strum across taut strings
stripped out from another toy.
When I'm all used up, the best bits
saved, throw away the carcass
the empty eyes and flayed flesh.
Bury me deep, broken back
and snapped legs I curl in on myself,
in years my flesh will fail and fade
and only your trophies remain.
If only I could feel the white anemone
above me, its petals marking
a grave site. Find me. Revisit me
and wonder if I know that you still
hold my fingers whenever you will.

Ren Warom provided:
Anemone, Spiral, Flute.

Ren Warom lives in Birmingham and is an exciting voice in the New Weird. Her novella *The Lonely Dark* was published by Fox Spirit in 2014 and her debut novel *Escapology* by Titan Books in 2016.

Remembered Hills

Holding hands they reach the peak
of a land they cannot claim as theirs –
a place of freedom far from the fighting.

The shoulder of a mountain lies back
and a llama picks across vacant homes,
between walls torn down and open.

Two women walk past glittering mines and
Spanish prayers – open air replaces stuffy
dinner parties on silver dug from beneath their feet.

Boots tread down the mud was raised
up. A lace petticoat below bright colours –
newly bought for a together life.

Someone hidden leads ahead, lighting an unseen
trail through steep forest. They carry all they need.
Fresh coffee, one teacup, cold cakes and matches.

The past looks warmer, it cannot last for anyone.
This view changes but the rocks we stand on
are stronger than we are. Built for a god.

Alex Bell provided:
Llama, Petticoat, Teacup.

Alex Bell writes novels and short stories for both adults and young adults, beginning with *The Ninth Circle* (Gollancz, 2008). Having determining to use her law degree for good rather than evil, she also works as an advisor for the Citizens Advice Bureau.

When shown "Remembered Hills", Alex commented: "Brilliant! What a gorgeous poem – I love it!"

The Dark Drop

It's narrowed to a tunnel.
Start to inch forward.
The ground tips, slowly
at first, fills with water.
Well. The light moves
overhead. High beauty
that I can't reach.
It has to be climbed to,
not crawled. Struggle up.
The walls have lies
written all over them.
They glitter, fresh
where nails have
marked out the letters.
If you read them
in the dark they look
like the truth. They turn,
twisted in spirals
to hold close against
my skin. Hope is a voice.
I can hear it, the vague
sound distorts as it drops
down. My feet are too numb
to climb, so I stay still,
getting colder while
the water rises around.

Brent Weeks provided:
Truth, Beauty Hope.

The Dark Prop $1.

Brent Weeks was born and raised in Montana, and now lives in Oregon with his wife, Kristi, and their daughter. He is the author of the best-selling Lightbringer and Night Angel series of novels, both published by Orbit.

Patchwork Dance

Folds of fabric fall as she
dances. Unheard music,
a life lived out inside her head.
The world trapped in the
cloth she carries. Cotton and
silk, seshweshwe, tartan
and taffeta. Her feet scuff
out a rhythm as she marks
her path. Her heels show
scratched commas and loose
words. A language to see,
not to know, never to be learned.

Lauren Beukes provided
Seshweshwe, Scuff, Commas.

Lauren Beukes is a South African novelist, short story writer, journalist and television scriptwriter. Her novels have won the Arthur C. Clarke Award, the Kitschies Red Tentacle (both for *Zoo City*), The Strand Magazine Critic's Best Novel Award, the RT Thriller of the Year, and South Africa's most prestigious literary award The University of Johannesburg Prize (all for *The Shining Girls*). Both *The Shining Girls* and her latest novel *Broken Monsters* have been optioned for TV production.

Fallen Palace

A rotten ballroom in a ruined state.
Books torn down for shelves – burnt for
warmth, fuelling so many fires.
Cold expanse of nacreous marble takes
your footprints and calls them back across
the court-yard. Curtains hang at half-mast
in long mourning of a grander purpose.
Bricks were built on top of bones,
with cruelty woven into foundations.
Revenge lit white, harsh and precise.
The untouched rooms, overlooked, hold
their history tight to their chests. Walls to
ceilings decorated by the delicate spinneret –
motions over years. A home re-claimed,
not for the people who needed change
but for something older. Spiders weave
where dust settles, covering un-loved beauty.

Chris Wooding provided:
Nacreous, Spinneret, Cruelty.

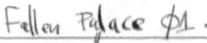

Chris Wooding is a British writer of science fiction and fantasy, with sixteen books to his credit which have been translated into twenty languages, won various awards, and been published around the world. He also writes for film and television, and has several projects currently in development.

V. C Linde

New Year's Eve

This liminal hour, this bordering day
the watched clock and the new page.
Another day like the last, to remember
our regrets, unchanged and unchallenged.
Promise a new start, promise hope,
let ourselves believe it all, just for one night.

We celebrate. Glasses meet halfway
to ring in the changes, shadows dance,
meeting before their bodies find each other,
chatoyant fireworks flash bright and linger
behind blinking eyes. The last spark is never
impressive, but quiet and sad. The let down
weighted by expectation. The effervescent hum
fades into a flat light of half-drunk champagne
marked with smudged lipstick. And then

after midnight
they carry on, as they always have.

We fall asleep before the light and dawn creeps
its winter breath down over the new year.

Rachel Neumeier provided:
Chatoyant, Effervescent, Liminal.

Rachel Neumeier is an American author of fantasy and young adult fantasy, including the House of Shadows series and the Griffin Mage trilogy, both published by Orbit.

Ex Nihilo

A void to start. Nothing to see and no one to miss
it.

Five children are born from the growing Chaos.
Night and Earth. Darkness and Love.
The Abyss.

The cosmos forms as their skin cracks
and falls into place across the vacuum.

The divine human – made from nothing –
the same as everything. Matters.
Each atom traced upwards, not back.
Built and born. Dirt and blood.
River mouth, table leg, needle's eye.

No guiding hand, no hint of the divine.
We are more real when our fathers
are made from the dust of earlier days.

Stephen Baxter provided:
Atom, Human, Cosmos.

Stephen Baxter has a degree in mathematics and a doctorate in engineering. He taught maths, physics and IT before becoming a full time writer. One of Britain's foremost science fiction authors, he has nearly sixty novels to his credit as well as five collections and nine chapbooks. He has co-written novels with Arthur C. Clarke, Terry Pratchett, and most recently Alastair Reynolds, and his work has won BSFA, Philip K. Dick, and Locus Awards.

Flash

Every burst of
light freezes the action and
keeps us in our place.

Damn any secrets,
We're caught in a moment,
kept. Always in view.

Day and night shown in
the camera's eye. So we
can remember this.

James Lovegrove provided:
Every, Damn, Day.

James Lovegrove is a New York Times best-selling author with more than fifty novels and books for children to his credit. He is also a respected reviewer of science fiction and of comics. He lives in Eastbourne with his wife and children

Behind The Lines

The weave of the needle
pulling flesh together,
draining the skin to a close.
Friperie torn from the Sunday
best, faded grandeur stained
with enemy blood.
A fight for money and land.
a fight for name and titles.
where to belong, who to follow.
The war a sequence of horrors,
in a new place with new graves
and heroes wishing they were
home. Again. The survivors fight
on, to the next slaughter.
Off to the side, further from
the smoke, another fight
plays out with soldiers already
wounded. The cruelty and chaos
follows them from the field.

Trudi Canavan provided:
Chaos, Weave, Friperie.

Trudi Canavan is an Australian fantasy author with two international best-selling series to her credit: The Black Magician trilogy and Age of the Five. She won her first Aurealis Award for short story "Whispers of the Mist Children" in 1999 and has never looked back.

Old Man Juniper

A view from the hidden side of a mountain,
nothing that happens is seen. No one tells tales
where the sun cannot catch flowers. One tree
grows, sideways out of the hills, rough and cruel.

The trunk's wide stance makes the land below it
darker, safer. A cold place to set down roots.

The thrawn tree holds the land in its grasp,
soil stays locked around it. Jackdaw pecks
the ground looking for anything to take back.
Her appetence the same for the unripe fruit
as for the fallen berries. The dark blue and
unfinished white. Stuck in the web of thorns.

Only one place to shelter. The house that
hides has two doors – safe and dangerous,
closed and open. The man within has one side.
Sharper than the tree outside. Not made but
changed, a construction of choices.
Shallow foundations hold weak walls.

Hal Duncan provided:
Thrawn Appetence, Stance.

OLD MAN JUNIPER #1.

Hal Duncan is a Scottish author of science fiction and fantasy who is never afraid to court controversy. A resident of Glasgow, he has two critically acclaimed novels – *Ink* and *Vellum* – to his credit and two collections.

Dorothea's Tomb

Cars scream by her bones,
buried underground by the
side of the road. A secret
shrine kept sacred. The walls
full of prayers, pleading
for help and guidance.
Mannequin dolls haunt the
scene. Figurines of her
living self. Before the saint,
the woman she was. Whole
and human. One part dead
and gone, her faith still alive.

Sarah Lotz provided:
Mannequin, Saint Underground

Sarah Lotz is an acclaimed writer of horror and dark thrillers; in addition to writing under her own name, she has written urban horror novels as S.L. Grey with author Louis Greenberg, a YA pulp-fiction zombie series *Deadlands* with her daughter Savannah under the pseudonym Lily Herne; and quirky erotica novels with authors Helen Moffett and Paige Nick under the name Helena S. Paige. Her novel *The Three* has been optioned by the BBC for TV production and S.L. Grey's upcoming thriller *The Apartment* has been optioned by Steven Spielberg's Amblin Partners for film adaptation.

Colonised

I never held a whip,
I never waved a flag
but the blood within me
carries the stain.

We didn't belong.

Pale feet sank into soft soil
when rains drowned the earth
growing lush forests to protect
the life led beneath them.
A verdant life, a bright home.
Skyscraping indigenous plants
twisted round, formed a labyrinth,
one path through. Know the way
and find the heart. Impatient we cut
a new path, straight and true.
A bypass, missing the point.

Our disreputable past lilts quietly
in the background, a chill counterpoint
to speeches made, to peace held inside
a handshake, to promises written
on burning paper.

Peter F. Hamilton provided:
Indigenous. Disreputable. Lush.

Peter F. Hamilton is one of Britain's most successful science fiction authors, noted for his epic space operas. He sold his first short story in 1988 and has gone on to enjoy worldwide sales of his novels in the millions. His best-known works include the Commonwealth Saga, the Night's Dawn trilogy, and the Void trilogy.

Major Arcana

The innocent sets out. Nothing and everyone.
Blind to the knowledge written on paved slabs
in front of him, not looking down but staring up,
he opens his arms wide – exposed, unprotected.
Safety off. Gaining momentum, one foot forward
towards an answer, away from a sound ignorance.

The ways are hidden, behind hedges, beyond sight,
over hills, concealed around corners, by everything
imagined in front of us, informed by everything
remembered behind us. Experience lies and
the route changes. The dice roll and cards fall in
new patterns. He sees an infinite number of choices
ahead. How to choose without understanding.
How to move without a map. The first word on a blank
page.
Faith and innocence on a painful road. We play the fool
and walk his path. Start from the same place.

Thorns under foot make thick scarred skin. Physical proof
of lessons learned. The dog at his feet bites his ankle,
a tearing rush to start out, get going, make a move.

Guy Adams provided:
Blank, Dog, Fool.

Guy Adams is a British writer now living in Spain. He is the author of The World House novels, the Deadbeat series and weird westerns *The Good, The Bad And The Infernal* and *Once Upon A Time In Hell*, while *The Clown Service*, his new series from Del Rey UK, mixes espionage with horror and fantasy. He also writes comics, including the forthcoming *Ulysses Sweet: Maniac For Hire* from 2000AD.

Unholy Night

The last nail
is forced from
the risen coffin.
The last dusk
has fled from
the clouded sky.
The last integument
was pulled from
the rotting soul.

Storm Constantine provided:
Dusk, Integument, Nail.

Storm Constantine is a British science fiction and fantasy author primarily known for her ground-breaking Wraeththu series, which challenges concepts of gender. She is the author of some thirty-five books, mostly novels but also short story collections and non-fiction volumes, and for the past thirteen years has run her own publishing business, Immanion Press.

Crash Barrier

Spin. Freeze-frame
the second they break through,
before gravity catches on.
Waiting.
Billowing glass hangs
barely outside the frame,
wavering steel flows like mercury.
Not long now.
Screams adjacent to silence,
caught in the back of the throat.
Move again. Time restarts. Fall.

Charlaine Harris provided:
Mercury, Billowing, Adjacent.

Charlaine Harris is a New York Times bestselling author who has been writing for over thirty years. Born and raised in the Mississippi River Delta, she first achieved publication in 1981 with *Sweet and Deadly*, but is best known for her novels about telepathic barmaid Sookie Stackhouse, which were adapted for TV as *True Blood*, premiering in 2008.

V. C Linde

Silvanus' Tapestry

His careful fingers twist the thread
to pull the rain through cloth of earth.

He stitches flowers, trees in silk,
the woodland colours come alive.

A constant work, season and year,
embroidered flora, stem and stalk.

Deliberate and delicate,
final and unfinished.

Adam Roberts provided:
Rain, Embroidered, Woodland.

On being shown "Silvanus' Tapestry", Adam said: "That poem is... extraordinary. Really beautiful and haunting. Wow! I'm not one to gush praise for no reason – really. Rather the opposite. But that is a stunning piece of lyric poetry."

Silvanus' Tapestry – 01

Adam Roberts is a British academic, critic, and BSFA Award-winning novelist. He has several score science fiction short stories and sixteen science fiction novels to his credit, most recently *The Thing Itself* (Gollancz 2015). He teaches literature and creative writing at Royal Holloway, University of London.

V. C Linde

The Birdcatcher

The cat and I stalked through the forest
of cages. Owls to hawks. Wrens to gulls.
I alphabetize by the sound of their song,
and we walk the calls from A to Z.
The cat's paws slide under a loose wire.
Kicking him away to foil his nefarious plot,
I tighten the fence to keep them safe
and sound.
A cacophony of canaries
A flurry of finches
A multitude of magpies
A pandemonium of parrots
A rabble of robins
A spiral of sparrows
I stay the predator, stalk the prey
and watch them beat their weakening
wings to a gridlocked sky
and criss-crossed clouds.

Kelley Armstrong provided:
Nefarious, Cacophony, Pandemonium.

Kelley Armstrong is a best-selling Canadian author of fantasy, horror and crime fiction, who has been writing tales of undead dolls and demons since her school days. Best known for her Otherworld novels, Kelley now has more than thirty books and a dozen chapbooks to her credit.

When shown "The Birdcatcher", Kelley said: "This is fantastic! She did a great job with three not-so-easy words."

V. C Linde

The Lethe Flows

She walks slowly past eternal fields –
rest beyond her banks, on the far side.

Hold her hands to your ear, listen to peace,
almost fall asleep as she sings and you hear dreams.

A daughter of discord, she fell far away and stood alone
hidden among memory. Stand still and see.

Choose where you walk – an easy path or not.
Travel only one way each time and forget again.

We live forever – preserved – with all our faults.
Knowledge kept, mistakes never unmade. One chance.

Everything can last. More immortal now than ever.
An image, a word, one click and it can return.

A river still flows but we cannot see why – should
we give it all back at the end of the dance.

Can we forget, if somewhere we are kept.
Can we change, if we choose to live forever.

Guy Gavriel Kay provided:
Almost, Memory, River.

Guy Gavriel Kay is a best-selling Canadian writer of fantasy fiction. His work has won Aurora, Sunburst, and World Fantasy Awards. Starting with the Fionavar Tapestry series in the 1980s, he has to date published thirteen novels and one book of poetry, while his fiction has been translated into more than twenty-five languages.

Manhattan

A long avenue runs straight
through the conquered isle.
Darkness where buildings scrape
the sky and keep out the light.
Old man sits in a damp doorway,
his broken hand tosses a coin
high. Casting his fate.
Damning theirs. Shell out for more
money. Gamble to gain
someone must always lose.
False lights from cars and shops
and neon signs make them forget
the night falling. The natural rhythm broken —
they bask in an artificial sun. The city
awake, unresting. Seasons not marked
by the length of the days but the length of a
hemline.
A collective unconnected they forget
to look back up to the hills.

Dan Abnett provided:
Coin, Darkness, Bask.

Dan Abnett has been writing comics and novels since the mid-1980s, including the Gaunt's Ghosts novels for Warhammer 40,000 and numerous titles for Marvel, DC, and 2000 AD. He is responsible for reviving many popular titles, including *Teen Titans* and *The Legion of Superheroes*, and he reinvented *The Guardians of the Galaxy* as the team subsequently featured in the Marvel films.

Drowned Out

Her body floats
hollow bones
drift away.
Bleached in the sun
as heat melts
all that she was.
No longer seen
as the face
that she wore.
Silence kept
by her
fading mouth.
This river her
grave.
The current her
rest.

Liz Williams provided:
River, Silence, Sun.

Liz Williams is a British science fiction and fantasy writer with the mind of a scientist and the soul of a Pagan. Perhaps best known for her Inspector Chen novels and the Winterstrike series, her work has been shortlisted for the Arthur C. Clarke and the Philip K. Dick Awards.

V. C Linde

Break/Down

Clench our fists and smash into
the view – an idyll frozen in a glass sphere.
We hold on as the world fractures
and the room explodes. We tip-turn upside-down.
A glass parakeet breaks his cage and flies
straight to the floor above. Free, we can fly away.
Where can we go? Lie down on the ceiling
as neurons fight the long war, an insurgency
to overthrow the rational thoughts. The bombardment
inside our heads – this chemical imbalance.
A carton of milk, soured by time and ignorance.
And the pills don't work well. And the bottle is empty.
And an epigenetic shift keeps memories whole.
And we talk and we talk and we talk.
Still the bird is free. Still the walls are gone.
Still the mould remains. Still we remain.

Charles Stross provided:
Epigenetic, Insurgency, Parakeet.

Charles Stross is a British writer of science fiction, fantasy, and Lovecraftian horror. Specialising in hard science fiction and space opera, he has produced some two dozen novels, two collections and ten chapbooks since 2001. His work has won Hugo, Sidewise, Locus, and Prometheus Awards.

V. C Linde

Road Map

I'm still the navigator when she knows
the route. Sow the seed and let the course
change with untrodden paths. I sit quietly
and watch where we go, glance back
to check that our memories are still safely there.
We find the wild ways.
Over unadopted roads and past pellucid lakes,
she decides and I agree. Our toes touch the edge
of the sea. Our fingers graze the side of the woodland.
Motorways rush past all of our favourite places, fast
but far from this. We dip away and wind through
the world in our own time.

Kate Elliot provided:
Navigator, Seed, Pellucid.

Kate Elliott is the pen name of American fantasy and science fiction writer Alis A. Rasmussen. Since 1990 she has been responsible for some twenty novels and a short story collection.

V. C Linde

Night Himself

Heavy hands still hold a trace of sonant red,
a lingering light cast by the retreating day –
deepest horizon hues show through his skin.
A hint of scarlet flickers, the last burning
before deep blue clarity walks over the world.

He marches steadily, gloaming feet dragging
along a willing weight, a dwindling flush
from his 6 am feet fades up into midnight eyes.

Dawn follows at a distance, matching his stride
but she starts late, never catching up.
The wakeful birds are charmed
by his sparkling smile. Eyes twinkle, the shape
of myth and legend, god and hero.

Kim Lakin-Smith provided:
Scarlet, Charmed, Gloaming.

Kim Lakin-Smith is a critically acclaimed writer of science fiction, dark fantasy and twisted realities for both adults and young adults. Her work has been shortlisted for BSFA Awards (twice) and a British Fantasy Award.

Princess

The perfect dress for a
fairy tale ending. Put on
costume and smiles. Low
lighting and high ceilings,
slow music and fast feet.
A night like so many others.
She's watched as a man
becomes a toad and many
frogs turn into princes. Bored
of the endless rounds she
keeps moving, dancing in a
construct free from conversation.
Whirled in a pulsing beat,
turning in the song spun
out as a high glissando
marks the end of the show.
She breathes, lowers her arms
and lets the story end, down
to earth with a bump.

Jeff Vandermeer provided:
Pulsing, Glissando, Toad.

Princess $1.

Jeff VanderMeer is an American New York Times best-selling writer and editor. He has won the Nebula, Rhysling, British Fantasy, BSFA and the World Fantasy Award (the latter three times), and has been a finalist for the Hugo Award. Renowned for his contributions to the New Weird, he is also the author of The Southern Reach Trilogy, the first volume of which, *Annihilation*, is currently in production with Paramount

Nest

High the trees
        near the clouds
               feathers warp and weave
        flocking together
    to hold safe the clutch.
Tucked in treasures make a house a home
Jackdaw
        Apple core
            Hawthorn
                Unborn.
Soft shell hardens
        Hoar frost melts
Harsh calls hold away
            a hunter in the cloud
    wings ghost overhead
            the gasp of air
between each beat, waiting, waiting, waiting
waiting for the
        crack of shell.
Watch the moon wane
        through an eddying sky
violet ink spilled onto black
        creeps into
    the fissure. Open.
Arrival. At last.

Jen Williams provided:
Ghost, Moon, Apple.

Jen Williams started writing about pirates and dragons as a young girl and has never stopped. She is the author of numerous short stories and the Copper Promise trilogy of novels.

Boarding Call

Minarets sing out, climbing the slopes
away from the docks. Sunlight vanishes
as a ship appears – high enough to make her cold.

One foot on the ladder and the world shifts,
fear grabs her ankles while the sea laughs at her.

She doesn't see the shore walk away, sitting down
to find an equilibrium. Her new school shoes echo,
moving slower than the waves that beat and grab
with passion, bringing ice hands up to meet her.

Her destination is only a name, a mystery
read about in books, spoken in quiet voices.
Her imagination forecasts rain and grey meals.

The waves below the ship scatter her reflection
and lull her to a new home and on the full-west
docks the sun will not greet her. Only a matron
and a starched uniform and English soil.

Sarah Pinborough provided:
Fear, Passion, Imagination.

Sarah Pinborough is a British writer of horror, fantasy, and near-future thrillers. Her work has been compared to that of Bentley Little, Richard Laymon and Dean Koontz, and has won her three British Fantasy Awards. She also writes for TV, and has several scripts in development.

V. C Linde

Exhibition

The street his catwalk, the route
planned, to see as he is seen.
Costume carefully in place, a show,
not the sublime he reaches out for
but only the ridicule he staged.
Each single step a baroque elaboration,
grand motions designed to exaggerate his form.
Shoulders pulled back, straight up
and down he stares ahead, keeping track
of his deliberate eccentricities.
Overstated, he hides behind
loud colours and brighter patterns.
Doors lock as he walks past, children
will stare, calling out in barbed laughter.
Maybe he can hear them.
Adults will mock in whispers behind his back.
Saying everything they think, they know.
A mess of desire. A strangeness he designed.
Nothing inside his layers of gold.

Ian Watson provided:
Baroque, Lock, Mock.

Ian Watson is a British science fiction writer now resident in Gijón, Spain. A graduate (with Honours) of Balliol College, Oxford, he is best known for his work with Stanley Kubrick, writing the screen story for *AI: Artificial Intelligence* (subsequently filmed by Steven Spielberg), and for being the first author to write in the Warhammer 40,000 universe. He has won two BSFA Awards and his novel *The Embedding* (acknowledged as influential by the likes of China Miéville) won France's Prix Apollo.

V. C Linde

Never Never Land

A shadow left behind to watch over, wait
until it sees a new child – ready to fly. Off.
Leave behind the sensible, the rules and order.
Archetypes walked this world before you –
know where the world drops away and pirates
attack, which boards to step and seas to swim.
His home held at the front of the mind,
while he never changes. The ebb and flow
of innocence all brought back with a touch.
Remember. Coloured paths lead us far
from home. Watch your children follow the path
and find the secrets hidden. In his mind,
they are all one – the first person – looking
to stay. Their feet grounded while his tear free –
leaving only a waiting ghost behind him.

Jaine Fenn provided:
Shadow, Mind, Flow.

Jaine Fenn is a British science fiction writer, best known for her Hidden Empire series of novels (Gollancz), starting with *Principles of Angels* (2008). Her short story collection *Downside Girls* (2012) features interlinked stories set in the same universe.

2 AM Café

The bouncer kept out the crowds, kept away the drunks.
Anyone who didn't fit, in, everyone who didn't belong.
Thirteen tables safe. She squeezed past him as he held
the door open for her. He smiled over her shoulder,
not looking even though she was wrapped
in one of her most outré outfits. Buzzed hair and sharp eyes
matched the electric thrum though her veins, the beat
of music pulsed where she had touched the night.
The heat of the never-dark city warmed her skin.

The waitresses weave, black uniforms shimmy
among the bright colours. Their lithe movement
around tables catches her eye as they dole out
pancakes and coffee, hot chocolate and late-night
breakfast, swerving to avoid wide gestures
and discarded trappings. Sweat held by hairlines,
behind knees and in high-heels.

The clubs had unloaded into the street where ghosts
of tables and tourists lingered. A fae tale of lissom limbs
and eager elegance taking back the tarmac. The queue
switched to this everlasting café. Only present
for a minute before the floors are swept
and everyone vanishes into the day.

She is tired, always moving on, now at rest.
Outside, Old Compton writhes towards a sleeping morning.
She watches the suits begin to arrive, her old life, her old
self.

Rod Rees provided:
Outré, Lissom, Shimmy.

Rod Rees is the author of the Demi-Monde quartet of novels, starting with *Demi-Monde: Winter* (2011), and also the short novel *Invent-10n* (2010).

V. C Linde

Paid With Interest

Hedges run along the path
"do not enter here".
Yet he ignores the warning,
walks straight past the signs.
Branches bend into a band
hawthorn cutting deep
to hold him still. Still.
He begs, mercy, calling out
salvation never comes,
his pleas lost to this forest,
hungry for his pulse.

The air grows still at midnight
when all debts are repaid
Flesh and thorns are drawn tight,
and bones to ground are laid.

Genevieve Cogman provided:
Mercy, Midnight, Hawthorn.

Genevieve Cogman is the author of the Invisible Library series of novels. She lives in the north of England, and for her day job she works as a clinical classification specialist. Her hobbies include patchwork, knitting, and role-playing games.

Leave A Comment

They hide behind screened names, meant to protect.
A mask to hide the attack. We're not pushed
and kicked anymore. Nothing left in the playground.

Broken armour. Start the chink and then it's easier
to twist the knife. An obvious riposte, watch the blade
fall in. Misspelled names, numbers shorten
the attack, coded insults we all recognise.

Call out. A note hangs, wavers. Articulated and clear,
Sticks and stones can't travel as far as words in the wire.

Passive voices clack down on distant keys.
Scuttling fingers drive the tanks into place.
Such a small action. Send. Out into the world.

Our actions last so long, remembered. Re-watched
and noticed. Information ages us while keeping us
running on the spot. Never get away again.

They found us – again. So run away. Hide away.
Keep trying to learn, if there is one place left to be safe.

Adrian Tchaikovsky provided:
Articulated, Scuttling, Riposte.

Adrian Tchaikovsky is the author of the acclaimed ten-book Shadows of the Apt series starting with *Empire in Black and Gold* (Tor UK). His other works include *Guns of the Dawn* and science fiction novel *Children of Time*, which is currently shortlisted for the Arthur C. Clarke Award.

Three Fold

Trip out to deeper waters, play the pirate
adventurer. Ocean under the deck, a bright
blue invitation to dance before the rains.
Three drops sink down onto an open palm.
Small feet twirl on soaked boards. Dance
through the day, making the dip and re –
rise of waves. A crystal night lets the planets align
in rare syzygy as a celestial storm fires our stars.
Lay back outside, and rock in motion.
Watch fish, bear, serpent, chasing
a corsair and her ship through the dark, lost,
too close to the stars to steer for safer waters.
Stitch the dreams together, with knotted braid,
an ethereal haberdashery to pull our thoughts
into shape, seen from this grounded earth.
A declining spectre drifting into relief.

Pat Cadigan provided:
Corsair, Haberdashery, Syzygy.

Pat Cadigan was born in the USA but she relocated to the UK in 1996 and now lives in London. Her work became closely identified with the cyberpunk movement, though this by no means defines it. Twice a winner of the Arthur C. Clarke Award, she has also won a Hugo and a World Fantasy Award.

When shown "Three Fold", Pat said: "I'm floored. Vick is an artiste. Seriously. That is an amazing piece of work."

Broken Lighthouse

A fleet of splinters,
planks scattered and
iron sinking into rust.
Sands shifting so far
below, letting sails settle
and rot. The light has
gone out above and
the moon only shows
the very top of each
wave crashing. An owl
screeches, the echo
of splitting wood,
and another boat slips.
Close to solid ground
but too near the shore.

Juliet Marillier provided:
Owl, Shifting, Fleet.

Juliet Marillier is a New Zealand-born writer of fantasy, focusing predominantly on historical fantasy. The author of some twenty novels and a collection, she is a four-times winner of Aurealis Awards.

Thy Servant Depart

Three people, then two, another couple, an old woman,
a tired man. They go slowly past oak tree guardians,
taking each step forwards into the South Porch, lost
to her eyes, as the darkness takes them in. Jostled by
the hurrying crowd, her bag slips and falls to the floor,
she stoops, kneeling. When she straightens up
the organ has opened the way, sounded the call
to prayer.

Tip-toe, trying to keep silent, trying to shut out
the questions. She sits in the quiet noise,
greedily taking up space with her shopping.
The day repeats in the swell of chords before her.

Awake but not moving, distanced from the day
and the crack of light haloed around borrowed
curtains, they sigh in and out with her. An arm
slung over her hips moves with her motion.
Lips stroke her skin, fingers kiss her. A morning
shift gets her up. Time passes with coffee
and complaints, listened and spoken. A wandering
afternoon, windows showing other lives and a lost
reflection that she barely owns yet.
Choices showing in her skin.

The Gloria Patri again. The gentle rise and fall.
The pattern comfortable. If she can still ask,
can he still forgive, will she know, question or answer.
A childhood spent in the same space, a different place.
Cities and towns all alike, under the roof the same
words sung unite people. The rules – call and respond.

Morning prayers to evensong, stay in the light,
too many questions in the darkness.

As the Creed, she stands, alone while others look
only forward. No need to be quiet anymore
her bags rustle and heads turn, she's not looking,
already facing the door and the dusky light waiting
for her in the darkening curiosity as night Falls and the
uncertain rules with doubt.

Paul Cornell provided:
Tree, Forgive, Evensong.

Paul Cornell has written Doctor Who for the BBC, Batman
& Robin for DC, and Wolverine for Marvel. He has won the
BSFA Award for his short fiction, the Eagle Award for his
comics, and shares a Writer's Guild Award for television. He
is one of only two people to be Hugo Award nominated for
all three media.

Hiber

A twist in the air,
as foliage turns
avocado to olive and rust,
camouflaging itself to the darkening year.
Time to rest, hedgehog and bat
sleep through
when owls hunt and ptarmigan forage.
Plants close and mammals sleep
but the weather is revivified,
breathe in rain, exhale fog.
Strong and sure, when storms roll through
crepuscular hours of twilight seasons.

Jack Skillingstead provided:
Crepuscular, Avocado, Hedgehog.

Jack Skillingstead is the author of two novels and a collection. He has been a finalist for both the Theodore Sturgeon Award and the Philip K. Dick Award. Since winning Stephen King's "On Writing" contest in 2001, he has sold more than forty short stories to major science fiction magazines and original anthologies.

Convergence

Four sisters met
at the cross-road.
One sister carried
a rose caught in thorns.
Two sister brought
a glim full of dark.
Three sister dragged
a dead flock of crows.
Four sister led
a pack made of fools.
Only one left
and three never were.

Mark Lawrence provided:
Thorns Fools Sister.

Mark Lawrence is a novelist of dual nationality (American and British), best known for his Broken Empire trilogy. In 2014, Lawrence won the David Gemmell Legend Awards for best novel for the first in the series, *Emperor of Thorns.*

Sampler

Needles prick
the pewter thimble,
match the holes,
mark the stitch.
A squamous pattern
shining in multi-
coloured patches.
She calls nature
down onto cloth.
A bird's cry, the bark
of the hounds and
snap of cold twigs.
Fingers work fast
and sure. Her nature
shown in sewn skill.

Tricia Sullivan provided:
Squamous, Thimble, Bark.

Tricia Sullivan won the 1999 Arthur C. Clarke Award for *Dreaming in Smoke*. Her other novels include *Maul*, *Lightborn*, and *Occupy Me*. A New Jersey native, she now lives in Shropshire with her family. She is an MSc student at the Astrophysics Research Institute.

V. C Linde

The Hanged Man

Run far from here, away from this
Turn your back on our crime
Let me carry the weight of guilt
Worry not for me this time

Look inside, look inside my love
And see what matters most
To have the rose, I'll bear the thorns
Sail rough seas to meet the coast

It wasn't greed, it wasn't pride
That drove us to this fate
It was justice for the hunted
Who were driven out by hate

Look inside, look inside my love
And see what matters most
To have the rose, I'll bear the thorns
Sail rough seas to meet the coast

We broke them out, smashed through the walls
Their souls again their own
And never more will we be blind
I will die, you'll live alone

Look inside, look inside my love
And see what matters most
To have the rose, I'll bear the thorns
Sail rough seas to meet the coast

You are safe, my heart, even as I hang
By the branches of the tree
The price is high but worth the cost
Oh, dying to be free.

Look inside, look inside my love
And see what matters most
To have the rose, I'll bear the thorns
Sail rough seas to meet the coast

The crescent moon sways by my feet
Dry leaves fall past my ear
I sit and wait to meet my fate
See the coffin and the bier

Look inside, look inside my love
And see what matters most
To have the rose, I'll bear the thorns
Sail rough seas to meet the coast

Their malice keeps them strong, my heart
Their power makes them cold
But if they saw how we see them
A cruelty deep and old

V. C Linde

Look inside, look inside my love
And see what matters most
To have the rose, I'll bear the thorns
Sail rough seas to meet the coast

Look away, look away my love
And see no more of me
To do what's right, I'll lose my life
But I will never lose thee.

Mark Chadbourn provided:
Crescent, Malice, Rose.

Mark Chadbourn is a journalist, novelist and script writer of BBC TV dramas. With some twenty novels to his credit, Mark is best known as a fantasy writer and has twice won the British Fantasy Award, but he has also written tie-in novels for Hellboy and Doctor Who.

Second Voices

Two steps left. Creak. And to the right. Creak. Shift the weight across. Creak. The house speaks its history to remind us that we do not own it. A visitor to this time only – owning each new second, never the next.

Ripped up floorboards are piled high by the staircase – an uneven mockery of purpose. And by the door frame, under the entrance is rosewood. Held by a hinge. It creaks open. The past shown to us in smug satisfaction.

Letters. One, Two, A lifetime. Sent into exile. The static voices predate actions spoken in the dust. Soft paper from listening so hard. She to He. Half a story, one side, half a life.

Pushed and pressed we hear them. A flower – given when – kept in waxed paper. A foil wrapping. A ticket torn. Gone. Or dead and still gone. Pulled up. A reassuring song from seconds long past.

Iain Banks provided:
Entrance, Foil, Predate.

Iain Banks (1954 – 2013) was one of Britain's most respected and successful writers, both within and outside of science fiction. The vast majority of his SF was set within the Culture universe. His work has been adapted for TV and radio.

Shown "Second Voices" in April 2013, two months prior to his passing, Iain messaged, "Loved the poem – please pass on to Vick."

Fail Better

Feel alive as you cut his skin,
blood gives you hope
that the next one will be better.

The last one you try will be right.

He failed you. The joyful light in your
eyes betrayed when he turned
out to be just like the others.
The wrong answers. He didn't say it.

Your nails crust, coloured and marked
by a life unworthy of your time.
Dead bodies at your feet, crowding
out the carpet. Walk away.

Find a new place, slip through the door
and never come back. Get lost
in the fog, watch it cover your steps
and move on. Keep searching.

Lou Morgan provided:
Hope, Joyful, Fog.

Lou Morgan is an award-nominated British author who writes both adult and YA fiction. Her first novel, *Blood and Feathers* was published in 2012 and the follow-up, *Blood and Feathers: Rebellion*, was released in the summer of 2013. Her first YA novel, *Sleepless*, appeared in 2015.

Trapeze

A split second
drop
as hands let go.

A moment to treasure

Unmeasured
by time or distance.

Watching in terror
safe in seats.

Falling in wonder
until the
next hand catches.

Tim Lebbon provided:
Wonder, Treasure, Terror.

Tim Lebbon's first story was published in 1994 and he became a fulltime writer in 2006. He has had some thirty books published in the UK and USA by a variety of publishers, including tie-in novels for both the *Aliens* and *Hellboy* franchises. To date his work has won four British Fantasy Awards and a Stoker Award.

V. C Linde

The Museum Of Things That Never Were

It's nowhere that you can see, it's never
been visited, hidden in the folds of a map.
A place full of the non-existent treasures,
kept in the attic of the cosmos. Under lock
and key. Safe because we know it exists.
An antediluvian apple tree, a snakeskin
purse holding a handful of silver coins.
Collected through time's imagination,
Nothing is real, none of it can be touched
or taken away. We can hold onto the idea,
a part of life that doesn't fade. A golden sheepskin,
a spear tipped with blood, a stone of eternal life.
A king sleeping, waiting. They never were
but they are real inside our beliefs.

Rachel Armstrong provided:
Antediluvian, Cosmos, Life.

Rachel Armstrong is Professor of Experimental Architecture at Newcastle University. Her practice is deeply involved in imagining and building new experiences and worlds and interrogating them through a variety of media. She innovates and designs sustainable solutions for the built environment using advanced new technologies such as synthetic biology and smart chemistry. Her first published fiction appeared in the anthologies *Paradox* and *Now We Are Ten* (both NewCon Press)

About the Author

V.C. Linde writes poetry and prose in the UK surrounded by piles of books, coffee mugs and a rebellious garden. In 2012 she won the New York Times Found Poetry Competition and since then her poems have been featured in both print anthologies and e-publications. Her début poetry chapbook and novella were published in 2014, but this book, *Just Three Words,* represents her first full collection. More of her work is available online at patreon.com/vc

www.ingramcontent.com/pod-product-compliance
Lightning Source LLC
Chambersburg PA
CBHW052009170626
46808CB00007B/2840